Hop's Case of Being Different

Text copyright © 2018 Keith and Cecile Michaelis

Illustrations copyright © 2018 Angie Savoy

All rights reserved. Published in the United States by the Live Like Noah Foundation

1st Edition, 2018 (originally written in 2011 by Noah Bella Michaelis at age 8)

Author: Noah Bella Michaelis

Illustrator: Angie Savoy

Cover by: Angie Savoy
(www.angiesavoy.com)

Presented by: The For The Win Project (www.forthewinproject.org)

For additional information on this book, the author, and the Live Like Noah Foundation,
please visit www.livelikenoah.org

Library of Congress Control Number: 2018912407
ISBN: 978-1-7325254-0-5

75% of the net proceeds from the sale of this book are being donated to The For The Win Project.

FOREWORD

We were driving home one evening and Noah asked to borrow my cell phone to record herself. She was fond of telling stories or singing on the voice memo app on my iPhone.

"I think I know what story I want to tell for the contest at school," she said. It was Fall 2011. Noah was 8 years old and in the 2nd grade.

I had forgotten what this year's theme was, so I asked her again.

"Diversity," she said.

Little did I know I would be gifted one of the most memorable experiences I've ever had with my daughter. And without skipping a beat, she began.

"Once there was a frog that lived in Frog Jumping Lake."

I sat quietly, driving home and listening intently, as she unwrapped this most precious gift of story complete with setting, character dialogue, and more impressively, a moral.

She painted such an incredible picture with her words—getting into character with each new friend she'd introduce. Nearing home, and feeling like Noah needed more time to finish telling her story, I decided to take a longer route so as to not disrupt her. I didn't want the story to end. I quietly asked myself, "How did she know how to craft such a beautiful story about diversity? She's only 8 years old." I remember feeling extremely proud, excited to have Noah share it with her dad.

At this young age, Noah was a book lover and make-believer; driven by stories that took you to another world, taught you lessons, cracked open mysteries, and solved problems. And while her imagination could run off with the stories she read, her body sometimes held her back. Noah was born with congenital heart disease and Heterotaxy Syndrome. By the age of five, she had gone through four open heart surgeries and had been in and out of the hospital most of her life for procedures or to just get over a cold that would often put someone like her in the hospital. But if you knew Noah, you would know she was someone who was most courageous, that when the going got tough, she got tougher. She was someone who never backed down from a challenge. This included committing herself to writing her story about Hop and to submit the story to a state-wide arts contest through school. Perhaps everything she had already gone through gave her the confidence to try anything.

At the time of submitting her story, Noah was receiving IV infusions at UCLA two to three times per week. Determined to get the job done and feeling incredibly proud of her short story, she wrote in long hand the last couple of pages while at the hospital as submissions were to be done in the child's own handwriting. As soon as she finished, her dad jumped in the car with it and drove all the way to Noah's school, which was in the very north end of the Valley, to make the submission deadline.

Several weeks later, Noah learned she not only won best literature for her school, but for her entire school district. And although she did not go on to win the statewide competition, this book is proof that will and fortitude can surpass all obstacles.

With Love & Kindness,
Cecile Michaelis

To Angie Savoy, Jesse Wilson, Jaimie Trueblood,

Hattie Eick, Jacqueline Fong, and Alison Gillis.

We couldn't have published this book without

your contributions and support.

–Keith and Cecile

For Noah

Love, Mom and Dad

HOP'S CASE OF BEING DIFFERENT

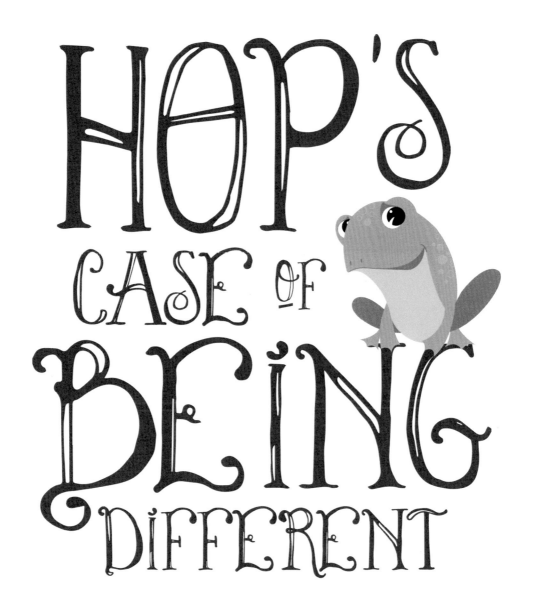

by
Noah Bella Michaelis

illustrated by
Angie Savoy

Once there was a frog that lived in Frog Jumping Lake.

The frog felt different from everyone else.

He always wanted to be a giraffe with a long neck
or a butterfly with beautiful magnificent wings,
or a tiger—big and strong.

Though, he was just a big, green blob.

The frog's name was Hop.

Hop liked to hop on every lily pad there was

and sometimes take a drink from the lake.

One day his friend Scarlet,
the butterfly, came to see him.

"Hello," she said in her magnificent light voice.
"Hi," Hop croaked. "Croak, croak, croak."

Scarlet asked,
"What's the long face for?"

"I wish I could be a big beautiful
butterfly like you," said Hop.

"Oh, you don't need to wish that. You are already beautiful. You are as beautiful as any butterfly in the sky."

"Really?" asked Hop.
"Really," said Scarlet.

"You should go hop over to Beauty the giraffe. She'll cheer you up. She's in the tall grass. You can't miss her."

"All right," said Hop.

As Scarlet flew away, Hop hopped from lily pad to lily pad over to Beauty.

"Hi," Hop said to Beauty.
Beauty had the same question as Scarlet.
"What's the long face for?"

"I'm sad," said Hop. "I want to be like you, tall with a long, long neck with those beautiful spots of yours."

"Oh, you are already beautiful. You're as beautiful as any tall giraffe.

You have something we don't have. You're special. You're different.

You have a very long tongue
that can catch flies.
Me, I prefer trees and don't
have that long of a tongue.
It's true," said Beauty.

"I know," said Hop.

Then Beauty said, "How about you go visit Razor the tiger. You always seem to have a great time with him."

So, Hop hopped over to Razor.

"Hi Hop!" said Razor.
"Hi," said Hop sadly.
"What's the long face for?" asked Razor.

"I don't like being different.
I wish I was as brave and strong as you," said Hop.

"Well, you're already strong and brave.
You are as strong and brave as
any other tiger here," said Razor.

"I know," said Hop.

"I know of a way to cheer you up! How about
I go walk you over to your old pal Sheller, the turtle?
He'll get you going!" said Razor.

"Okay," said Hop.

So, Razor and Hop went over to Sheller.

Sheller was basking in the sun.

Razor roared, "WAKE UP!"
And Hop croaked, "CROAK!"

"AWWWW!" Sheller said surprisingly.

"Sorry we had to wake you up. It's us," said Razor.
"Poor Hop has the bad case of being different. He doesn't like being different."

"Well," said Sheller, "You are diverse, basically."

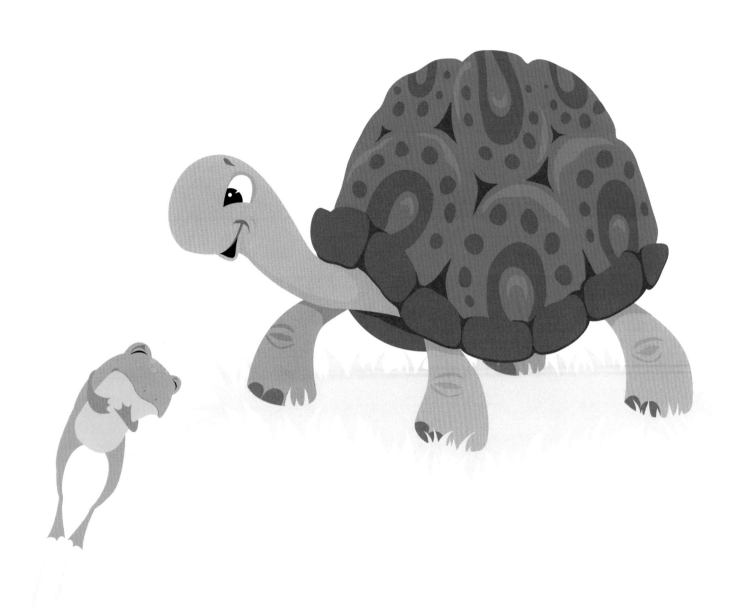

"I'm not diverse. I'm Hop—a frog that catches flies!"

"Oh, I'm not talking about you. I'm talking about, well, the way you look. You look like a frog, right? And I look like a turtle, correct?" Sheller asked.

"Yeah, of course I know that," said Hop.

"Well, your body is very diverse from mine, which means it's different than mine," said Sheller.

"But I don't like being different! I do not!" said Hop.

"Look at Razor and me. We are both different.
I have a short neck and he has stripes.
I have a shell and he doesn't.
See, everyone's different and it's okay.
Everyone's diverse.

I have a friend who's an
African tortoise and lives in Africa.
Well, he has an accent. We may look kind
of the same but we are also different.
Everyone's different," said Sheller.

"Think about it. By each of us being different, we can learn from one another, and that's fun!"

After this, Hop felt much better

and was hopping
on lily pads

and jumping in the water.

Hop liked being different.

THE END

ABOUT THE AUTHOR

Noah Bella Michaelis, an inquisitive and precocious young lady, whose love for fantasy and faraway places moved her to write stories inspired by Mary Pope Osborne, author of the Magic Treehouse series; Carolyn Keene, author of the Nancy Drew series; and Sir Arthur Conan Doyle, author of the Sherlock Holmes series.

Aside from being a gifted 7th grader, Noah lived daily with Congenital Heart Disease. She was born with a single ventricle as a result of having Heterotaxy Syndrome. She survived four open heart surgeries by the age of five and endured several other procedures and hospitalizations throughout her life.

Noah lived a life full of grace and grit, humility and compassion, humor and spontaneity, despite the complexities of her medical needs. She sought pleasures in the simple things. She taught us fear is what gives you guts, and having guts gives you perseverance to get through it, allowing you to see the light at the end of the tunnel. At 13 years old, Noah mastered life's challenges and gifted her knowledge onto all she knew and, unknowingly, to so many who didn't. We are all wiser for it.

Noah Bella was born on November 7, 2003, lived in Los Angeles with her parents, Keith and Cecile, and her big pup and tortoise, Finn and Escher. At the age of 13, multiple complications stemming from her CHD overtook her life and Noah passed away on January 3rd, 2017.

75% of net proceeds from the sale of this book are being donated to The For The Win Project

The For The Win Project Mission:

Since 2015, we have been giving seriously ill, disabled, and disadvantaged children the opportunity to be their favorite heroes. The For The Win Project is a 501(c)3 approved charitable organization that gives children in special circumstances the chance to be their favorite heroes in their very own "official" movie poster & trailer. In doing this, we create a new sense of hope, motivation, and self-esteem boost for each child. Transforming them into celebrated, larger-than-life champions will be influential in raising both awareness and funds for whatever they may be up against. Real life superheroes fighting the most important fight of all…the fight for their lives. There are so many kids out there that deserve better. In response, we developed this mission. It's called The For The Win Project. Because everyone deserves a chance to win, be awesome, and feel awesome.

Jesse Wilson and Jaimie Trueblood
Co-Founders of The For The Win Project
www.forthewinproject.org

Noah's The For The Win Project Experience:

Noah's The For The Win Project experience started off with a photoshoot at UCLA Mattel Children's Hospital complete with costume, lighting, and a wind machine for that cool windblown hair effect. This was just the beginning, Jaimie and Jesse, the co-founders of The For the Win Project, told us. Their mission is to give kids, with special circumstances, the chance to be their favorite hero in their very own epic poster and to create an experience from the initial photoshoot to the poster reveal. They transformed Noah into "Darth Noah" as Noah liked how Darth Vader was tall and physically strong, something she was not. The reveal, in November of 2015, was an unforgettable experience with friends and family, Ewoks and R2-D2, stormtroopers, and yes, Lord Vader. The poster was signed by Princess Leah herself, Carrie Fisher, who left an endearing message to Noah. Jaimie and Jesse not only transformed Noah that day, but transformed her thoughts, as well as ours, of the last few years of medical struggles; 2-3x weekly medical infusions, having a PICC line for 22-months, several hospital stays—into something of the past. That reveal day marked the beginning of new memories and stories, the feeling that anything is possible. The experience will forever be part of our lives.

Keith and Cecile Michaelis (Mom and Dad)

"Darth Noah" Poster Reveal, November 2015

Made in the USA
San Bernardino, CA
03 December 2018